I0706274

INTO THE STORM

SHANE KROETSCH

Into the Storm

Copyright © Shane Kroetsch

First edition April 2020

Pencil on Paper
Airdrie, Alberta
Canada
www.pencilonpaper.ca

ISBN 978-1-9994820-4-6 (paperback)

ISBN 978-1-9994820-5-3 (ebook)

Cover design by Francois Vaillancourt

CONTENT WARNING

This story contains scenes of graphic violence and death, gore, and gun violence, as well as a scene that alludes to sexual assault involving a child.

This is for the misfits and the misunderstood. Give yourself permission to share your gifts. Show the world what it means to shine.

ONE

The girl sat with her knees tucked under her chin and her arms tight around her legs. She looked to the boy kneeling across from her. His head was low, so it did not rub against the loose row of shirts and sweaters hanging above him. Shadows masked one of his eyes, the other held faint light coming through the slats on the closet door.

The girl tilted her head, and her mousy brown ponytail flipped to one side. "Who's turn is it again?"

"It's yours." The boy's voice could barely be heard. "I told you."

The girl frowned. "Okay."

She unwrapped her arms and balanced herself on the fake wood paneling of the back wall as she brought her feet under her. Her knees made divots in the thick, burnt orange carpet. She let out a deep breath as she looked around the cramped space. "I spy with my little eye, something that is…green."

One corner of the boy's mouth turned down, and the freckles on his cheek shifted. He twisted his body side to side and looked high and low.

"It's a good one. You're never going to get it."

The boy paused and pointed up. "Is it Dad's shirt? The one with the zombie face on it."

The girl shook her head. "Nope."

"That umbrella back in the corner?"

"Nope." A smile crept across the girl's face. Her blue-gray eyes brightened.

The boy tilted his head back and looked up into the mess of clothes above his head. He pushed a hand through to fan them out. He stopped between a short summer dress with an intricate pattern and a charcoal gray work shirt with a patch on the chest that read 'Fort Erie Electric'. "What about Mom's dress? The one with the white flowers?"

"That's teal, not green."

"So, that's a no?"

"That's a no. Keep guessing."

"I've already had three guesses. Just tell me already."

The girl giggled. "Okay, fine. It's your *eyes*."

The boy frowned and shook his head. "My eyes are hazel, not green. And how am I supposed to guess that when I can't see them?"

"What was I supposed to do? We've already guessed everything else."

"Whatever." The boy looked through the vents in the closet door. "Keep it down a little, okay?"

The girl frowned. "Sorry." She reached out in front of her and picked up a fabric doll with a hard plastic head and wild, stringy blonde hair. She held it close to her and leaned her cheek against it. "Can we go now?"

The boy lowered his head. "No. Not yet."

"What are we going to do then?"

"I don't know. What do you want to do?" The boy held up a pointed finger. "Don't say tea party."

The girl's shoulders dropped. "Oh."

On the other side of the door, a sound like distant thunder echoed. The boy straightened his back and looked up. The girl kept her focus on the doll as if she had not heard a sound. "I wish we could watch TV."

"Yeah, me too."

"My friend Sophie says she doesn't get to watch TV because she's always at dance class or piano lessons. Her parents make her go to bed early too." The girl wiped at her nose. "She has her own computer. I wish I had my own computer."

"What do you need a computer for? You're only nine."

The girl shrugged. "Games and stuff."

"Yeah, but you don't *need* it."

"But I want it."

The boy rubbed at one eye. "Yeah, well, I want a lot of things too, but it's not the same thing."

"Christmas is coming. Maybe Santa will bring me one."

The boy pushed air out of his nose. "Good luck with that."

"You always ruin my fun."

"It's hard to ruin something if there's no chance of it happening."

The girl puckered her face. "Just 'cause you're older than me don't mean you know everything."

"Maybe, but it means I know a lot more than you."

From outside the closet came the muffled sounds of raised voices and a door being slammed.

The girl ran a hand over the doll's head and whispered. "Still, you don't know it all."

"Nobody knows everything, not even scientists."

"Do too."

"No, they don't. Otherwise, why haven't they cured cancer or figured out how to stop tornadoes."

The girl shrugged and looked away. "I don't know."

"Exactly."

The two sat, not looking at each other. The voices outside became more urgent. Their exchange punctuated with a thud and breaking glass, then a woman screamed.

The girl's voice wavered. "Tell me a story or somethin'? Please?"

The boy rubbed the flats of his hands down his legs. "Okay."

He cleared his throat. "So, there was two kids. Brother and sister, like you and me. They both had bunk beds, not because they had to share a room, but because they lived in such an awesome house, and their friends always wanted to stay over. They had all the fun video games, and a swimming pool, and a trampoline in the backyard. Their mom walked them to school every day or drove them when the weather was bad because they didn't ever want to be late. They got good grades and made their parents proud, so they got to eat whatever they wanted for dinner, even if sometimes it was breakfast."

"How many dolls did the girl have?"

"Like, a hundred. More than anyone else she knew."

The girl smiled.

The boy opened his mouth to continue but stopped. He could feel someone stomping down the hall outside of the room. A man's voice growled. "Boy? *Get on out here.*"

The boy's lips were thin and tight. He raised a single finger to them. The girl's eyes went wide, and she clutched her doll tighter.

A door along the hall burst open. "Where are you, you little piece of shit?"

The boy held his hands over his head and rocked back.

Footsteps stormed into the room. First, a dresser drawer slammed shut, then the footsteps came around the bed.

A woman's voice, on the edge of tears, came from the open door. "Everett? Just come on back to the kitchen, and I'll get you another beer. Okay, baby?"

The boy heard two heavy steps, the impact of a calloused hand against soft skin, and a grunt followed by the sound of a body sliding down the wall.

"Stupid bitch."

The footsteps came in front of the closet door. The boy motioned for the girl to push back into the corner.

Tears streaked down the girl's cheeks, and she nodded. She closed her eyes and sank into the pile of clothes behind her.

The closet doors rocked back on their hinges. A figure stood silhouetted against the single bulb hanging from the middle of the ceiling. The man loomed with his arms wide at his sides. He wore an undershirt and a pair of khaki pants. The white socks on his feet were thin, and one of his big toes poked out. Thinning, dirty blonde hair stuck up from his head, greasy and unkempt. He smelled of sweat and the sweet sting of alcohol. Even in the shadows, the boy could see the man's face, red like lava and damp with perspiration. His mouth spread wide in a snarl, and a bit of spittle stuck at the corner of his mouth.

"There you are, you little son of a bitch." The man reached into the closet and took a handful of sandy hair. "Get your ass out here."

The boy cried out and wrapped both hands, small and pale

in comparison, around the man's wrists. The man pulled the boy across the room as his feet fought for purchase. The man paused at the bedroom door with his hand on the frame. He cleared his throat between sharp breaths, then looked back to the woman still sobbing on the floor. He swallowed and stumbled out into the hall with his jaw hanging low, the boy struggling in his grasp.

———

In the backyard, Della stood with her hands in her pockets and the hood of her coat pinched around her face. A stray wisp of hair flipped back and forth across the bright red tip of her nose.

She faced the bushes growing in the far left-hand corner where two sections of broken wood fence met. She watched the branches resist the wind as dead leaves fell and tumbled away. A framework of two upended pallets had been set in among the overgrown shrubs. Strapped together with weather-beaten coiled rope, the contraption had a slight lean. A tattered baby blanket hung from the edge of a third pallet, bridged across the top. It was only half effective as a door. Della could see the bucket with a crack in the bottom that had been upended as a table and one of the neighbor's patio chair cushions that blew over the fence the summer before. One of Della's own pencil crayon drawings had fallen from the wall and rested in the dirt. Another had curled out from the makeshift wall, a rusty nail stuck through it still holding it secure.

Della wiped at her nose, then stuck her hand back in her pocket. "Jason?"

A quiet voice came from behind the blanket. "What?"

"Are you okay?"

"Yeah."

"Okay."

Della watched the blanket shift in the breeze and waited.

"Dell?"

"What?"

"Do you ever think about when we'll be old enough to leave?"

Della sniffed and lowered her head. "Sometimes."

"Me too."

The wind gusted. Two houses down, a dog barked.

"That's a long time from now, though."

"How old do you think you need to be?"

Della shrugged. "I don't know, like, a grown-up."

The voice behind the blanket spoke in a whisper. "Maybe."

"It's just, you have to have a job and everything. Plus, kids can't buy houses and cars."

Della waited for a response, but it didn't come.

"Jason?"

"Yeah?"

"Are you sure you're okay?"

"I don't know."

Della wiped at her nose again. "Mom says you need to come in. It's time for bed." She heard a response, but it was little more than a whisper. "What did you say?"

"I said okay."

"All right. I'm going in. It's cold." Della turned and took two steps. She paused to look back but saw no sign of her brother, so she continued on.

The door to the house clicked shut. Eyes peered out from behind the blanket, and a small, pale hand pushed it to one side. Jason spun his body, so his feet stuck out of the makeshift fort. He paused to look at the backpack pushed up against the wall of twisted branches and tall, dying grass. The gray accents were all but indistinguishable from the black fabric of the body. He let out a deep breath, then shimmied clear of the bushes and stood.

Jason brushed his hands down the seat of his pants. He looked at the house, and his heartbeat rose into his temples. The glow from the living room window skipped and flickered with the action of the TV screen. Jason brushed the hair from his eyes, careful to avoid the shadow of a bruise across his right cheek, then blew warm air into his hands and walked up to the back door.

TWO

Lori set a bowl brimming with frosted oat circles and a dribble of milk down one side onto the table. "Morning, baby. How'd you sleep?"

Jason pulled out one of the four chairs and sat hunched forward. He yawned as he rubbed at one eye. "Morning, Mom. Okay."

Lori smiled and fanned her fingers out. "It's Friday, so that's something at least."

Jason stuffed a spoon heaped with cereal into his mouth and mumbled his response. "I like school, though."

"I know, baby. You're lucky that way. I always hated school."

Jason readied another spoonful and looked up to his mother. Her ash brown hair had been pulled back in a loose braid, and her cheeks were tinted with blush. "Is Dad home?"

"No, he had to head in early." Lori took a packet from the kitchen counter and tapped out a cigarette.

"Are you going out tonight?"

"Just for a bit. I'll pick you guys up some burgers on my way home from work. You'll be fine."

Lori moved to the kitchen sink and reached up to pull the sliding window open a crack. She snapped down the button of a small plastic lighter, held the flame to the end of her cigarette, then blew smoke toward the window as she peered up to the sky. "Looks like it's going to snow." Lori turned and rested against the counter with the cigarette held high and the opposite hand cradling her elbow. She inspected her manicure as the smoke drifted up. "Be sure to put on a warm jacket."

Jason nodded. He finished his cereal in silence, then took his bowl and put it in the sink. On his way back, he stood close to his mother and wrapped his arms around her waist. "Love you."

Lori looked down and set her cigarette on the black plastic ashtray beside the kitchen sink. She wrapped her arms over Jason's shoulders and rested her cheek on top of his head. "Aww."

Jason leaned back, and Lori held his face in her hands. She kissed his forehead and smiled wide enough that her chipped tooth showed. "I love you too, baby." Lori stepped back and lifted the smoldering cigarette from the ashtray. "Now go tell your sister to hurry up. You're going to be late for school."

———

Everett walked through the front door and dropped his work bag on the floor. He bent down to undo the laces of his boots, then kicked them off onto the boot mat.

Lori stood in the kitchen with her arms crossed and a lit cigarette in her right hand. The ashtray behind her overflowed with crooked butt ends. She gnawed at her bottom lip, and her face lacked color.

Everett scratched at the notch on his chin and watched her as he walked past to the fridge. "What's wrong with you?"

"It's Jason. I don't know where he is."

Everett pulled the fridge door open and leaned in. He came out with one hand wrapped around a can of beer and the other lifting the tab. "What do you mean you don't know where he is?"

"He's not here. That's what I mean."

Everett tipped the can to his lips and flipped the fridge door closed. He wiped at his mouth with the back of his hand and stared at the floor. "He's probably at a friend's house."

"That's what Della said too. I called around. Nobody knows where he is." She bounced a leg and took a drag from her cigarette. "Hell, a couple I called told me that Jason and their kids don't even hang out anymore."

Everett looked down the hall. He stepped back, set his beer on the kitchen table, and walked to the first bedroom door. Jason's bed sat along the left wall. The wrinkled blue comforter had been hastily pushed into place. White sheets with a race car design hung down to the floor. The bed in the far right corner had a pink unicorn comforter balled up near the headboard with a one-eyed teddy bear propped against it. Della laid on her belly with her feet in the air on the carpet between the two beds. She colored on a stack of lined binder paper with a purple crayon. When she noticed her father standing in front of her, she stopped kicking her legs to the song she was singing to herself.

Everett leaned his forearm against the doorway. "Where's your brother?"

Della tightened her grip around the crayon. "I don't know."

Everett pursed his lips. "Did he come home from school?"

"No. When I came out of class, he gave me the key and said he was going to a friend's house."

"Which friend?"

"I don't know. He didn't tell me."

Everett stood back and looked along the hall. "You know what happens when you lie, right?"

Della swallowed, then she nodded.

Everett turned his eyes to the girl and watched a moment, dropped his hands, and walked back to the kitchen.

At the table, he stopped to pick up the can of beer. It was empty by the time he made his way to the sink. He belched and tossed the hollow can into a garbage bag tied to a drawer handle. "Get dressed. We're going out."

Lori stammered, "What about Jason?"

Everett leaned forward with his hands grabbing the edge of the sink basin. "He's a big boy. I'm sure he'll be back by the time we get home. Better be anyways."

"No, I—"

Everett turned and ran a hand back through his hair. "I said get ready." He reached into his pants pocket, stepped in front of Lori, and pushed a small plastic baggie into her hands. "I got you a little something."

Everett walked away, and Lori looked down at her hand. She sniffed and closed her fingers tight. With a shaking hand, Lori turned to crush the end of her cigarette. She wiped at the corner of her eye, then followed Everett down the hall to their bedroom.

———

A young boy in jeans and a blue striped shirt ran to the end of the basement stairs and hung off the end of the banister. "Nico, Mom says it's time to shut down. It's dinner time."

Nico sighed and dropped the game controller on the floor beside him. "Okay."

The young boy turned and stomped back up the stairs.

Jason looked to Nico and set his controller down as well.

Nico uncrossed his legs and pulled the white tube socks from his feet. He pushed the cuffs of his long-sleeved t-shirt past his elbows and stood.

Jason sat on his knees. "Do you think it's still okay if I stay?"

Nico shrugged. "Sure, just have to ask my mom."

Jason nodded. He looked down and pulled at the loose skin on the back of his hand.

Nico walked to the TV and turned it off. "Come on."

Jason stood and followed Nico upstairs.

Nico's mother balanced a stack of plates on one arm as she set them out on the table. Nico came up beside her and put his hands in his pockets. "Mom, can Jason stay over tonight?"

Nico's mother stopped. She looked up, seemingly at nothing, then turned to Jason. "I suppose so. It's been a while since you had a sleepover." She looked down and set the last plate out, then brushed her hands down the front of her pants. "As long as it's okay with Jason's mom."

Both Nico and his mother looked toward Jason. His eyes moved back and forth between them. "She said it was okay, but I can double-check if you want."

Nico's mother walked to the kitchen counter and lifted a cordless phone from the cradle. She held the phone out to Jason. "Just to be safe."

Jason nodded and took the phone. He used his thumbs to

enter the number, then looked up. Nico stood staring off at the TV in the living room. His mother had moved along the counter to take cutlery from a drawer. Jason pressed the end button, then held the phone to his ear. In his mind, he counted *one, two, three, four.*

"Mom? Is it okay if I stay the night at Nico's?"

One, two, three.

"Oh, I have my gym strip. I can sleep in that."

One, two, three.

"Okay, see you in the morning. Bye."

Jason pressed down on the end button again and stepped over to the counter to replace the phone on its cradle. "She says it's okay."

Nico's mother gave a thin smile. "All right then, I hope you like lasagna."

———

Jason laid on the carpet with a thin pillow under his head and a fleece blanket flat across his chest. The blanket smelled like lavender.

A wooden nightstand with a single drawer and open bottom was at his head. The pleated plastic shade on the lamp sitting on top lit a bright, round spot on the ceiling. Jason watched the bands of light and shadow radiating outward from it.

"Do you think we can play more in the morning?"

Nico laid on his side with his arm bent and his hand pressed flat against his head. The neck of his t-shirt was stretched out and had a hole at the collar. A blanket tucked up just under his chest. "I don't know. I don't normally get to play on electronics until after lunch."

"Oh."

"Don't you have that game?"

"No, we don't have a system. Dad says he doesn't want it in the house."

"What do you do for fun then?"

Jason shrugged. "I don't know. Ride my bike. Play games with my sister."

"Like what?"

"We make stuff up mostly. Tell stories sometimes. We have a fort in the backyard that we hang out in."

"Sounds fun. My dad won't let us build anything like that."

"It's not a big deal."

Nico shrugged one shoulder.

Jason turned to look at Nico. "Do you hang out with your dad much?"

"Sure. I mean, sometimes. He takes us out to the lake all the time. We go skating once in a while in the winter. We even went to a Leafs game last season. What about you?"

Jason looked away. "Not really."

"He doesn't ride bikes with you or anything?"

"I don't know if he's ever ridden a bike."

"Like, ever?"

"Maybe when he was a kid or something. I've never really thought about it."

Nico wiped at his nose. "What's it like having a sister?"

Jason rolled on his side, facing Nico. He could see a dirty sock and a couple crumpled sheets of paper under the bed. "It's okay."

"Does she bug you a lot?"

"Sometimes. She likes to talk a lot too. Especially when I'm trying to go to sleep."

"Why don't you just lock your door or something?"

"We share a room."

Nico scrunched his face. "Really?"

Jason looked at the carpet and wiped his hand along the plush, beige fibers. "Yeah."

"That sucks."

Jason shrugged. He squeezed his lips together and pushed a quick breath out of his nose. "What's it like having a brother?"

"It's okay. He follows me around a lot and wants to do whatever I'm doing. Sometimes it gets annoying."

"Yeah."

"You know what's really annoying about brothers?"

"What?"

Nico smiled wide. "When they rip farts and then try to blame it on you."

Jason giggled. "What?"

Nico sat up in bed and fanned his covers. "Oh my God, Jason, why would you do that?"

Jason covered his face with his arm and made choking noises as he rolled away. "That's disgusting."

"It really is. Maybe you should go see a doctor or something."

Jason laughed. Nico laughed, then he farted again, which sent them into a roaring crescendo of cackling.

Nico wiped a tear from his eye. "Sorry, it happens every time Mom makes lasagna."

The bedroom door opened a crack. Jason flinched and turned at the sound of the hinges moving. Nico's laughter faded. He looked at Jason, then to his father, who leaned into the room.

"Lights out, you guys."

Nico coughed and smiled. "Okay." He reached out and pulled the chain on the lamp.

The room faded into gray shadows. Jason pulled the fleece blanket over his shoulders and closed his eyes.

———

Della laid in bed with the comforter pulled to her chin. She watched the shadows play across the ceiling as snow fell, and the neighbor's tree moved in the glow cast by the streetlight at the front of the house. Every now and then, the wind would gust and rattle the cracked pane in the window.

Her eyes fluttered, threatening to close, then the front door unlocked and snapped open. Della looked to the empty bed on the other side of the room and tightened her grip on the comforter.

Stumbling and slurred words came from down the hall, then her mother's laugh, low and sighing. The commotion moved closer, and two shadows passed by Della's open door. Everett scraped the wall. Lori remained upright only because Everett had one arm tucked under her shoulders. One of her feet could not gain traction and dragged behind her as they went.

They continued past the bathroom, then the door closed at the end of the hall. Della rolled onto her side to face the wall and shut her eyes.

A curious dream woke Della sometime later. She drew in a deep breath, and her eyes fluttered open. The room was gray. Snow ticked against the window. Down the hall, a stream of liquid let loose into the toilet bowl. It tapered off and ended with drips on the porcelain rim and floor. The lid slammed down. Someone cleared their throat, then shuffled out into the hall and toward her room.

Della rolled to face the door, hoping for Jason's silhouette in the dim light. The shadow eclipsing it was someone much taller than her brother, though. She closed her eyes and laid still.

Dragging footsteps moved into the room and stopped beside her bed. Fingernails scratched against skin, chasing an itch away, then the air stilled for a moment. Her mattress shifted with a weight that drew her small body toward it. Heavy, irregular breathing washed over her. It smelled of stale cigarettes and hard liquor. Della let her lips crack open and inhaled a slow breath through her mouth.

She kept her eyes closed tight and counted her heartbeat as it echoed in her head. Before she reached the number ten, chill air swept down her back. The comforter dragged along her nightgown and settled below her waist. Warm, calloused fingertips traced from the base of her neck, down her arm and to her side. They stopped at her lower back, then the full weight of the hand rested on her hip.

The fingers constricted and relaxed in small movements. The weight on the bed shifted, and the stink of acrid breath drew close. Della tensed but fought the urge to call out. The hand began to move up to her ribcage, pushing her nightgown along with it. She shrugged her shoulder and pressed her head into her pillow as if she was moving in her sleep. The hand stopped, but the heaviness stayed. Three more heartbeats and the squeal of tight hinges sounded from down the hall. Her mother made a small moaning sound, then coughed, wet and deep.

After a sigh and another brush of breath, the hand lifted from her body, and the weight tilted away.

Dragging footsteps moved up the hall. Della cracked one eye and watched a figure pass her door, heading toward the kitchen. A cupboard door clunked shut, and the faucet ran. Della heard water being gulped down and a glass click against the plates stacked in the sink.

The weight lifted from Della's bed, and she swayed forward. Footsteps moved from beside her bed to the hall. At the same time, bare feet on linoleum moved back from the kitchen.

"What are you doin'?"

The shadow in Della's doorway leaned against the frame. "Just takin' a piss. You still feelin' alright?"

Della's mother let out a breath as if to laugh. "Yeah."

The shadow turned and walked down the hall. Lori followed close behind.

After her parent's bedroom door closed, Della drew in a deep breath and pulled her comforter up to her face. One hand emerged to wipe at the tears tracking down her cheek, and her body shook as she stifled the sobbing rising in her chest.

THREE

Della stopped at the entrance to her parent's bedroom. She put one ear against the door, then reached up and turned the knob. Through the sliver of the opening, her mother's arm dangled along the side of the bed. The rest of her body remained hidden by the covers. The lump of blankets beside her rose and fell with her father's deep breathing. Della stepped into the room with her comforter over her shoulders and trailing behind her on the floor.

"Mommy?"

The hanging arm twitched, then pulled back under the covers.

"Mommy, I'm cold."

Lori groaned and moved the cover from her face. She brushed a hand across her forehead to move the wild tangle of hair from her eyes. "What's wrong?"

"It's cold."

"So, turn the thermostat up."

"I tried."

"Then go grab another blanket or something."

"But Mo—"

"*Go back to bed.*"

Lori pulled the blanket up above her head and rolled over.

"But, Jason—"

Lori sat bolt upright and pointed a sharp finger toward the door. "For Christ's sake, Della, get your ass back to bed."

Everett rolled over and opened one eye. Della lowered her head and turned to walk down the hall.

She sat in the middle of the living room floor with her comforter pooled around her, raised the TV remote, and pressed the power button. The screen stayed dark. She pressed it again, but the result did not change. Della held the remote up and shook it in front of her face. She tried one last time, then set the remote beside her and looked around the dim room.

A loose-knit blanket had been left balled up in the corner of the couch with a romance paperback open face down on top. An old picture of a mountain surrounded by trees hung crooked above it. A plant sat on a wire rack by the big window facing the backyard, its leaves brown and thin.

Della frowned, and her shoulders slumped forward. She looked toward the kitchen and wiped her nose.

She pushed the comforter off her shoulders, jumped up, and shuffled into the kitchen. She pulled a bowl down from one of the cupboards and took a spoon from the drawer below. After setting them on the table, she turned back to grab a box of cereal from beside the toaster. The inside of the fridge was dark, but she hardly noticed. Della took the milk carton out in one hand and eased the door shut. She poured the milk into her cereal and picked up the bowl with both hands. With her eyes wide and focused on the shifting load, she walked back to the living room.

Della bent forward and set the bowl on the floor. She spun around and sat cross-legged inside the circle left by her comforter, then pulled it up over her shoulders. Being careful not to spill a drop, she picked up the bowl and raised a spoonful to her mouth while watching the falling snow through the living room window.

———

Jason sat up and rubbed one eye. "What's wrong?"

Nico yawned and sat forward. "Power's out."

Nico's mother walked into the room with a pile of folded blankets balanced in the crook of her arm. She tossed one onto Nico's bed and held another out for Jason. "Take these and stay warm. We're still trying to figure out what's going on."

Jason took the blanket and spread it out over himself. "Thank you."

Nico's mother arched her eyebrows and turned toward the door. "Be back soon."

———

Lori walked down the hall with one hand weaving through her tangled hair and the other held along the wall to guide her. She stopped to use the bathroom and stuck her head into the kid's room. Both beds were empty, so she continued on to the kitchen.

When Lori opened the cupboard where the drinking glasses lived, it was empty. She looked down to the sink and dug through the stacks of dirty plates until she found a glass that seemed halfway clean. Lori ran her thumb and finger along the rim, then filled it with water. She drained the glass and set it back in the sink.

A quiet sneeze came from the living room. Lori walked in to see Della bundled up on the floor with a box of crayons and a stack of paper. Della looked up but quickly focused back on her drawing. "Morning, Mom."

"Morning, baby. Where's your brother?"

Della stopped drawing. Only her eyes moved. "I don't know."

Lori crossed her arms as the remaining color left her face. "What do you mean you don't know?"

Della's lower lip trembled. "I don't know. I tried to tell you."

Lori's eyes went wide, and she brought the palm of her hand to her forehead. "Oh no…"

She moved on unsteady feet to the kitchen. Lifting the phone from the wall, she pressed the buttons. The line was dead. Lori tried the talk button three times, but it did not respond. She spun to her left, then right. She flipped the light switch up and down, but the room remained dim. "No, no, no."

Lori sped down the hall to her bedroom. She found her purse under a pile of clothes and ran a hand through the contents until she found her cell phone. The no service icon lit up in the corner.

She moved around the bed to the opposite nightstand and reached for Everett's phone. His arm shot out and grabbed her wrist as she tried to pull it back.

"What the hell are you doing?"

"I just need to check your phone. I've got no service."

"So, use the house phone."

"It's down too. So are the lights." Lori dropped the phone

and stepped forward to place a hand on Everett's shoulder. "It's Jason. He didn't come home yesterday."

Everett released his grip and rolled to his back. He stared at the ceiling and sighed. "Son of a bitch."

"We need to go look for him. *Please.*"

Everett ran a hand over his face. "If he wanted to be home, he'd be home. He probably stayed over at whatever friend's house he went to."

Tears filled the corners of Lori's eyes. "He's twelve years old, Ev. What if he's hurt? I mean, it's snowing, he's probably cold—"

"Whatever he is, it's his own damn fault." Everett rolled over again to face the middle of the bed. "Why the hell is it so cold in here?"

"Are you even listening? The power's out."

"Whatever. I'm goin' back to sleep, then."

Lori stood back with her arms straight by her side, her fists clenched. "Damnit, he's your son."

Everett adjusted his body and pushed his face deeper into his pillow. "Prove it."

Lori opened her mouth to speak, but the words stuck in her throat. She wiped at her cheek and bolted from the room.

At the front door, she stuck her feet into her shoes and took a coat from the hook on the wall. She opened the door, and a pile of snow poured onto the floor mat. Lori clenched her jaw and kicked at the snow, clearing a path onto the front step.

Her car was parked closest to the stairs, encased in a prison of formless white. Only the windows of Everett's work van showed. She looked beside the door for a broom or shovel but found neither. Over the fence, in the back corner of the yard, she saw the peak of the shed heaped with snow.

Lori walked down the porch steps to the low gate bordering the yard. She pulled up on the latch and leaned into the gate, but she could not get traction to open it enough to squeeze through.

Lori swore to herself and kicked her way back to the front of her car. She tucked her hands into her sleeves and swiped them across the hood. With every armful of snow that she pushed away, more cascaded down to replace it. Lori stepped back to catch her breath and look at the situation, then leaned in and doubled her attack with clenched teeth and tears running down her cheeks.

An old truck, with a rattle can spray job and a home-built topper, labored up in front of the house. Lori watched as the driver stepped down and came around the front of the truck and up the drive with a slow, deliberate pace.

The man was stocky with long, wiry gray hair and a full beard. His dark eyes were half-hidden behind tanned and wrinkled skin. His nose was round and pockmarked. Every bit of his clothing held grease stains and had worn through in spots. The plaid jacket he wore frayed along the bottom, and his baggy jeans rode low on his waist. Stopping beside Lori's car, the man slid his hands into pockets.

"Mornin'."

Lori wiped at her eyes. "Hey, Mel."

"You ain't really plannin' on tryin' ta drive that thing outta here, are ya?"

"Yeah." Lori looked toward the house. "I, uh, need to go to the store."

Mel pushed the crooked bill of his cap up and scratched the top of his head. "You won't make it. Hell, I barely made it here locked in four-wheel drive. Some of the main roads got a plow, but not the neighborhoods. Besides, town's pretty much shut right down. Ain't no power anywhere that I can see."

"Oh." Lori squeezed her hands together and looked at the snow sticking to her pajama pants.

"What's wrong with you, then?"

Lori raised her head and smiled through fresh tears. "Nothing. I just really wanted to go to the store."

Mel frowned and pushed his jaw to one side.

The door of the house opened, and Everett leaned out. "Hey, Mel."

Mel raised a hand and pushed his way to the front door. "Hey there, nephew."

"What are you doing out here?"

"Can't do nothin' but stare at the walls, so figured I'd stop by for a beer or three."

Everett waved him on. "Come on in."

Mel pulled himself up the steps and slipped past Everett into the house.

Everett watched Mel as he went by, then looked to Lori. "What the hell are you doing?"

Lori looked out to the street. "We need to go look for Jason."

"We don't need to go do nothin'." Everett looked up into the falling snow. "Especially right now."

"But, Ev—"

"Get your ass back in the house. We've got a guest." Everett stepped inside and slammed the door behind him.

Lori stared at the closed door. Snow continued to fall, and so did her tears along with it.

———

Nico's father walked past the entrance to the living room, stepped back, and leaned in. "How are you guys holding up?"

Only Nico looked up. "Good."

Nico's father scratched at his chin. "Jason, maybe after lunch, I'll see if we can get the car dug out and get you home. I'm sure your parents must be worried."

"It's okay. I can walk home."

"Have you looked outside? It's a full-on blizzard out there."

Jason shrugged. "I brought warm clothes. It won't be bad."

Nico's father raised his eyebrows and frowned.

Jason smiled. "I'll be okay, I promise. I love the snow."

Nico's father sighed and tapped a finger against the wall. "All right then. Lunch will be ready in about ten minutes. It's not much but will keep us going at least."

Jason fought to keep the sadness from his eyes. "Thank you, Mr. Meyer."

Nico's father nodded and walked on.

———

Everett craned his neck and leaned forward. "Babe? Why don't you grab us some beers?"

On her way back from changing out of her wet clothes, Lori opened the fridge, stacked a can on another, and took both out with one hand. Walking into the living room, she held one out.

Mel reached up to take it. He cracked the tab, sat back, and spread his legs out. "That's what the neighbor told me. Military came in, and they closed the border on the US side.

All hell's breaking loose, man. Probably why the power's out too."

Lori sat on the arm of Everett's chair and handed him the second can. Everett pulled the tab back and scowled. "Fuckin' government. Probably ain't nothing at all. Any excuse for them to waste our money."

Mel grunted and took a swig from his beer.

Della walked into the living room wearing her coat and had a second pair of socks pulled up over her pants. "Mommy, I'm hungry."

"Go grab a granola bar or something."

"But there aren't any."

"What do you mean? I just bought a new box."

Della shrugged.

Lori sighed and rubbed her forehead. "Okay, let me see what I can figure out."

Della watched her mother.

Lori made a shooing motion with one hand. "Go on. I'll call you when it's ready."

Della frowned and lowered her head, then walked to her room.

Lori lowered her chin to her chest. "All right." She lifted herself to standing and walked toward the kitchen. Lori stopped in the middle of the room and bent down to pick up a crayon that Della had left behind. Looking back from the corner of her eye, she saw Mel watching her. His eyes were half closed, and one hand was deep in his pants pocket. It moved along the inside of his leg, slow and rhythmic.

Lori stood straight and pulled down on her sweater, then smoothed a hand along the leg of her yoga pants. She looked away from Mel, her cheeks full of color, and walked out of the room.

Mel sat up and finished his beer. "Well, I best get home to the old lady, make sure she ain't froze to death."

Everett laughed. "You should be so lucky."

Mel shrugged. "Could be worse." He smiled and nodded toward the kitchen. "Could be better too."

Everett leaned forward on his elbows. "Yeah, well, appearances can deceive."

Mel stood, limped over beside Everett, and laid a hand on his shoulder. "I'd pay good money for a fine ass like that to deceive me for a few minutes."

Everett lowered his eyes and shook his head. "Maybe next time."

"All right, then. Stay warm."

"You too, Mel."

Mel gave a sloppy salute and walked out the front door into the snow. Everett tipped his beer back to drain it and squinted out the living room window. He heard Mel's engine roar to life, then settle into a rough idle. Everett squinted out the living room window as the truck struggled its way down the street.

———

Jason stopped near a row of trees that ran along the side street at the end of his block. He set his backpack on the snow and opened the top. Digging around inside, he found and pulled out a small plush penguin. Jason stuffed the penguin into the top of his jacket, then zipped up his backpack and pushed it behind one of the trees. Hopping through the deepest snow, he moved up the edge of the street and into the alley.

Two lines of tracks ran down the middle. A few houses in, someone had attempted to shovel a path out. The blanket of snow was otherwise pristine, and Jason stood alone. He moved along the tracks but veered off and stopped at Mr. and Mrs. Duffy's house. He unlatched the gate and grunted as he leaned on it to gain a gap wide enough to squeeze through.

Jason crept under the bushes along the fence line. Snow had encapsulated the shrubbery and created a dark tunnel. Crawling through the broken boards, dividing the properties, he shimmied into his own backyard.

He crouched down in the corner and watched the house. Once in a while, he would catch glimpses of movement through the living room window, but nothing more. Laying on his belly, Jason crawled along the fence. He slipped under a gap in the bushes and pushed through the weeds into the dark sanctuary of the pallet fort.

He scanned around the blanket door to be sure he would not be spotted. The clamor of a revving engine with a bad muffler made him jump. With his back against the sidewall, he took a deep breath and wiped at his nose with his forearm. He pulled at the zipper on his jacket, then removed the penguin and a folded piece of paper. After arranging them on the upturned bucket, Jason sat on his knees and turned to go back into the bushes. One of Della's drawings had fallen, so he picked it up and stuck it to a nail on the opposite wall. He wiped his nose again, then pushed back through the weeds and branches and snaked out into the alley.

———

Everett scraped the side of his fork along the plate in front of him. He licked the thin tomato sauce from it, set the fork down, and leaned his forearms against the table. The plate in front of Della sat untouched. Everett picked at his teeth with his tongue and looked at the girl. "Eat your dinner."

Della sat on her hands with her shoulders hunched. Hair hung in front of her eyes and obscured them.

"What's the matter? Not good enough for ya?"

Della crossed her arms. "I'm not hungry."

"Eat your goddamned dinner. You ain't going anywhere until you do."

Della tightened her arms and stuck her lower lip out.

Red filled up Everett's face like a thermometer. He slammed his flat hand on the table, then stood over Della. He pointed and jabbed his hand toward the plate of canned spaghetti and screamed inches from her ear. "I work hard all fuckin' day to pay for this, so you're not gonna fuckin' waste it, you ungrateful little bitch."

Lori stood and held out a hand. "Ev, come on."

Everett turned away with clenched teeth and his hands on his hips. He stood staring and shaking, then spun and drew back an open hand. Della cried out and held her arms over her head. Bringing his hand down, Everett flipped the plate into the air and onto the floor. Spaghetti and shards of cheap porcelain shot out in all directions.

"There, you happy now?" Everett kicked his chair away, took his glass from the table, and turned to walk away. He stopped to open the cupboard door over the fridge, pulled down a half-empty bottle of whiskey, then went on into the living room.

Lori rose from her chair and knelt beside Della. She put an arm over the girl and rested a cheek on her shoulder. "It's okay, baby. It's okay."

Lori wiped away tears of her own while Della sobbed.

When her breath leveled, she stood. "Go on to your room. I'll get this cleaned up."

Della sniffed and wiped an arm across her face. She looked up to her mother with watery eyes, stood, and ran to her room.

———

Jason climbed up from the ditch and pointed east. He would not have thought to walk on the road on a normal day, but it was a welcome respite from wading through the deepest sections of snow. Some streets had been plowed, but few sidewalks were clear. Jason took the easy paths when he could, but he did what he needed to do to avoid any people he came across on his journey. He had seen one car on the road that morning and a handful of others stuck or slid off to the side.

When he came to the boulevard along the river, he turned south. He turned his gaze to watch the way the gulls blended in and out of the monotone gray sky and falling snow. The river pushed through it all, dark and powerful. He stopped when the Peace Bridge came into view. Two police cruisers parked across the outbound lanes with red and blue lights flashing. Jason swallowed. He looked around and behind him, adjusted the strap of his bag, and focused back on the bridge. On the nearest side, a line of transport trucks waited to cross the border by the blockade. Two big yellow diggers worked to clear the snow.

On the far side of the river, the situation looked worse. More lights and vehicles. Some appeared to be military. People on foot gathered back from the crossing, but they were too far away for Jason to understand why. Small fires had been lit to help keep people warm. Thin columns of smoke could be seen further back toward the city.

Jason looked away from the bridge and along the road to the next intersection. He walked up to it and headed west, away from the commotion.

———

Lori knocked on the plain wood door, turned the knob, and walked into the room. Della sat on her bed with the pink comforter draped over her head. She held it closed under her chin, giving her the look of a Russian stacking doll. Her eyes remained fixed on the floor.

Lori cleared her throat and sat on the end of Della's bed. She held out a sandwich on a folded piece of paper towel. "It's peanut butter and grape jelly."

Della moved her eyes to the sandwich, then back to the floor.

"Come on, Della. It's your favorite."

Della tightened her grip on the comforter.

"It's just…this is hard on all of us, the power out and everything." Lori looked across the room to Jason's empty bed. "You know how Daddy can be. Things will be better in the morning, right?"

Della adjusted her position and turned away from her mother.

Lori frowned and looked down at her hands. She sighed, stood, and set the sandwich on the small pink table at the head of Della's bed. "Eat up, then brush your teeth and go to bed. Please."

Lori crossed her arms and watched Della. The girl didn't

move, so Lori left the room and eased the door closed behind her.

———

Jason moved from the main road into the opening of a wide service road. He stepped through the snow around a wood power pole and rested against it. Leaning forward with his hands on his knees, he drew in and pushed out a deep breath.

He stood upright and scanned the road. Past the dumpsters and stacks of old pallets, it curved off to the right and out of sight. Before the curve, he saw a gate held closed with a heavy chain. A gap in the gate looked wide enough for a twelve-year-old to squeeze through but not much more. Jason adjusted the straps on his backpack and trudged on through the snow.

When he arrived at the chain-link fence, Jason grabbed at the wire and leaned forward to look through. He saw no sign that anyone had been around since the beginning of the storm. The lot was closed in on two sides. Heavy steel racking, filled with metal bars and pipes, lined the back wall of the building beside a tall roll-up door. The man-door had a metal bar across with a heavy keyed lock to secure it. Next to the door, a nine-pane window with a corrugated metal awning over the top. A cube van with flat tires and crude graffiti sprayed on the box sat next to piles of old, rusty machinery along the brick wall, separating the yard from the boat repair business beside it.

Jason pulled on the gate to test it. The chain had been looped snug, but years of too-sharp turns and backing up without looking had bent the posts enough to stop it from closing tight. He took off his backpack, pushed it through, then crouched down and slipped into the yard.

After shouldering his backpack, Jason took slow, high steps to the driver's door of the cube van. He let out a sharp breath and wrapped his fingers around the door handle. He pressed the button with his thumb, but it stuck halfway. When Jason tightened his grip and leaned into it, the mechanism released, and the door popped open a crack. Rusty hinges groaned as he pulled it open. Inside, the bench seat had a slip-on cover that was dirty and coming apart at the seams. Curled yellow papers and empty take-out coffee cups littered the dash. An old food can, propped against the transmission hump, overflowed with stale cigarette butts, and heaps of garbage and crumpled plastic bags covered the floor.

Jason put his foot on the sill of the door and lifted himself up to kneel on the seat. He swept his arm across to clear it, then took his backpack off and pushed it to the passenger side door. Jason paused and looked to the sky. A band of light, visible to the west, began to fade. Snowflakes drifted down from the darkness above him. Jason sat back on the seat, reached for the handle, and closed the van door.

FOUR

Della's shoulders sagged. "But, Mom, I don't want to."

Lori held up a puffy coat by the hood and tilted her head. "Please, Della. It's only breakfast time, and you're already getting on my nerves."

"But I'm *bored.*"

"I know, baby, I know. I wish there was more I could do, but there's not. For both our sakes, please, just go play outside."

Della reached out and swiped her coat from her mother's hand. "Fine."

She slipped her arms into the sleeves and stomped to the back door.

Lori chased after her. "Don't forget your mitts."

Della glared at her mother, took her mitts, and dropped them on the floor. She sat, pulled her boots over her feet, put on her mittens, and stood.

Lori sat down at the table and lit a cigarette. Della stuck her tongue out at the back of her mother's head as she zipped her coat up, then walked out to the backyard.

Della kicked at the snow on the first step, sending small pieces cascading down to the untouched sea of white. Raising her feet high, she stomped down the steps and out to the middle of the yard. She spun in a tight circle and trampled the snow to a hard crust. Even after she stopped, the world continued to spin. Della closed her eyes and shook her head. When she opened them again, her balance returned. Next, she kicked to loosen the snow and shoveled it away with her hands. She kept at it until a space twice as wide as she was had been cleared. Satisfied with the size, she held her hands out from her sides and dropped into the hole.

Della hunched forward and held her eyes just above the snowline. Great clouds of vapor puffed out with each breath. Her lips puckered, and her eyes narrowed in a stern gaze. She scanned the yard toward the house like a soldier in a foxhole. Her breath rose and swirled away. With no sign of enemy combatants, she pushed the hood of her coat back and pulled the zipper down from her chin. She shimmied around to face the opposite direction, then hugged her knees to her chest.

The back side of the yard was equally stark. Snow piled high over the bushes in the corner. A small bird flew along the top of the fence and up the alley, chittering as it went.

Della focused on the front of the fort. Through the gap at the door, she saw the corners of her pictures lifting ever so slightly in the breeze. She looked to the house, then back to the drawings.

Della stood and brushed at her knees. Pulling back on the cuffs of her gloves, she started digging. At first, she moved in big sweeping motions, then like a dog paddling through water, and finally scooping armfuls to the side.

Standing in front of the fort, she pushed her bangs away from her face with the back of her hand. Della drew in one deep breath and slowly let it out, attempting to relax her racing heart. When it had settled to something resembling a normal rate, she knelt down and pushed through the blanket door.

The inside of the fort was dim. Della looked to the ground, where she remembered her picture being last, then up to where it hung on the wall. She crawled around the perimeter, watching the plush penguin standing on the upturned bucket. Its eyes seemed to follow her as she went. Della backed into the far corner. The weeds along the back had parted with some of the stalks bent or broken, and bits of snow had been tracked in on the floor.

She directed her eyes to the penguin and the piece of paper it held down. The shadows in the plastic eyes were unmoving yet somehow alive. Leaning forward, she adjusted her position and lowered her hand. With her thumb and forefinger pinched on a corner of the paper, she wiggled it back and forth until it broke free.

Still watching the penguin, she unfolded the paper and held it up. Her eyes moved to the page and scanned the words written in hasty block letters. A smile came to her cold lips. She read it twice more before setting it down.

Sitting back on her heels, Della's eyes darted around the fort but focused on nothing in particular. Her lips pinched and moved to one side, then she picked up the paper again. She folded it in half and began to put it in her pocket but paused. With her free hand, she grabbed the penguin and slid it into the open top of her coat, as she had seen Jason do so many times before. With the penguin secure, she tilted the bucket back and set the note underneath. Della cinched up the zipper of her coat and turned to face the door. "Come on, Waddles. Let's go inside and warm up."

Jason formed one last snowball and set it down with the others. He sat with his back flat against the wall he had worked most of the afternoon to build. Looking over his shoulder, he stretched out his fingers and smacked his hands together to shake off loose snow. Finally, he settled back down and hunched low.

"Okay, boys, we've got bad guys incoming. Let's do this thing."

Jason rolled onto his knees facing the snow wall. He stacked three snowballs in the crook of his left arm and held a fourth in his free hand. He looked to his left, then to his right. "On my count. One, two—"

Jason popped up from behind the wall, shouted out with his teeth bared, and started throwing. First, he targeted a sign on the chain-link fence with a picture of a video camera, then a pile of steel barrels stacked up beside. He reached down to restock his arm and turned to his left. He pointed and bellowed in a deep voice, "We've got tanks incoming."

The next four shots hit the windshield and front wheel of the cube van. Jason followed them with a series of impressive exploding noises. He jumped up and waved his hands, celebrating his victory. "We did it. *We did it.*" He hopped from foot to foot and pumped his fists. "Good job, boys. Let's go home."

Jason kicked at the remnants of a poorly formed snowball, then dropped to sit against the fort wall. He pulled off his gloves and wiped at the corner of his mouth. Staring out across the yard, he sighed as he thought about home. He wondered what Della was doing and if she was keeping warm.

A snowflake fell through his line of sight. Jason tilted his head up to the gray sky and listened. The world around him was quiet, save the rustling of the wind. It did not seem that his antics had been enough to distract anyone from their struggles.

Jason lowered his head and reached for his backpack. After digging around the bottom, he took out a granola bar, then peeled off the wrapper and dropped it in the bag. He bit off a third of the bar and scanned the yard while he chewed. Shadows grew longer, highlighting the tangled, congested space. The thought of spending a second night among the sharp bits and precariously stacked debris did not appeal to him. The truck smelled funny too.

He popped the rest of the granola bar in his mouth and pushed the rolled-up blanket to one side of his bag. Two more bars sat at the bottom next to a brown banana. He lifted out an empty pop bottle but left a half-full bottle of iced tea leaning inside. Jason felt along the front pouch and pinched his fingers around the outline of a juice box. He took the empty bottle and walked to one of the last remaining untouched patches of snow in the lot. Jamming as much snow into the tiny opening as possible, Jason tightened the cap and stuffed it in his jacket pocket.

Picking at a rogue piece of oat from his teeth, Jason leaned forward with his hands flat on the snow wall of his fort. The granola bar had not done much to satiate his hunger, and the grumble from his stomach confirmed it. The next road over would take him down to the plaza with a grocery store, two fast-food places and a proper sit-down restaurant.

Jason stepped back and scanned the ground to ensure he had collected all his belongings, then lifted his backpack by the top loop and slipped an arm through one strap. "Good job today, boys. Couldn't have done it without you."

He walked across the yard, squeezed through the gap in the chain-link fence, and moved on down the road.

———

Della sat on the edge of her chair, leaning over the kitchen table. One hand held the top corner of a sheet of paper. With the other, she used a pink crayon to fill in the cheeks on the face of a doll with button eyes. She hummed to herself under her breath.

Lori walked into the kitchen with her arms crossed tight. She had a coat on over her sweater. Her hair was tied back in a ragged ponytail, and the skin around her eyes was creased and puffy. At the sink, she turned and rested her back against the counter. She watched the table as she reached out for the packet of cigarettes and lighter next to the sink. "Is that yours?"

Della did not look up to the plush penguin sitting on the table in front of her. "No, he's Jason's. His name is Waddles."

"Why did you bring it out here?"

Della sat back, eyed her drawing, and shrugged.

Lori pulled air through the end of the cigarette and exhaled toward the ceiling. "We all miss him and are worried about him, but he's going to be okay. You know that, right?"

A thin smile came to Della's lips. "I know."

Lori cocked her head and raised an eyebrow. She held her cigarette up between two fingers and examined Della's face. "Good." She took another drag and set the cigarette on the rim of the ashtray. "Do you want a snack before bed?"

Della shook her head. "No, I'm okay."

Lori walked to the fridge and opened the door. She examined the sparse shelves and sighed. The door thumped shut as she went back to the sink and filled an empty glass at the faucet. Gazing out the window, she watched the waves of snow drifting from the sky. She took a sip from the glass but recoiled from the flash of pain as the cold water washed over her teeth. Holding her hand to her lips, she set the glass down on the counter.

Lori leaned back against the counter and crossed her arms again. A single tear broke loose from the corner of her eye as she stared at the penguin on the table.

———

Jason stepped into the trees, holding one hand out to balance on low branches as he went. The snow was not as heavy under their dense cover, so walking became easier. At a spot near the middle of the small grove, he set down his backpack and squatted up against a tree trunk. Jason could not see the road to the south or the houses he knew sat to the north. In fact, he couldn't see anything in the dim light past the edge of the grove itself. His heart raced as his eyes moved from tree to tree. It reminded him of a haunted forest in a fairy tale. He repeated to himself that he could be out in thirty seconds if he needed to.

Dark, patchy bark peeled off the trunk of a fallen tree nearby. Bare branches splayed out and obscured a hollow underneath. Jason poked through the twigs and dead leaves with one foot. No bugs, mice, or subterranean monsters emerged, so he crouched and crawled behind the branches. He pushed his backpack off to one side near where he would lay his head. Watching what snowflakes were able to break through the canopy, Jason held his arms tight around his body. For a moment, he wished he had not left Waddles at home.

When he pictured Della finding him, he knew it was the right decision though.

Dusk settled. Jason kept his head down and pushed himself further under the near-horizontal tree. He pulled his backpack onto his lap and opened the zipper to the main compartment. After taking out the rolled-up blanket and a frozen pack of hamburger buns he had retrieved from the grocery store dumpster, Jason surveyed the remaining contents. The iced tea bottle was empty, the bottle of snow had not thawed enough to be of much use, and only one granola bar remained.

Jason zipped his pack, folded it in half, and set it on the ground. He pushed the blanket to unroll it, then flipped it out to open it up. Leaning back, he stretched out his legs under the tree and pulled the blanket over himself. He fussed for a moment to kick the end of it under his feet and body to form a polyester cocoon. For a time, he laid still, watching the last of the light fade.

———

Jason's eyes fluttered. He tilted his head up and looked into the darkness. As he set his head down on the backpack pillow, sounds of commotion came from the direction of the crossing. At first, it was like a stadium full of people booing a missed shot on net. It rolled and grew, then it began to change. He sat up and focused on the noise over his heavy breathing and pounding heart. Individual words were impossible to make out, but Jason recognized anger when he heard it.

A dull pop rang out. Then another. The tone of the crowd shifted toward urgency and fear. A continuous volley of gunfire rolled through the air, punctuated by the thud of an explosion. The volume of the voices grew. Soon, even the sound of the river was overtaken. Metal impacting metal, bending and breaking, came next. The voices turned to screams.

Jason held his hands over his ears and rocked back and forth while he searched through the woven branches of the trees for some hint of the night sky above. Under his breath, he repeated a lullaby his mother used to sing to distract him from a bad dream, or his father's wrath.

Twinkle, twinkle, little star,
How I wonder what you are,
When the song ended, he would start again.
Up above the world so high,
Like a diamond in the sky.
Over and over, it looped through his mind.
Then the traveler in the dark,
Thanks you for your tiny spark,
He repeated it so many times that individual words started to lose meaning.
He could not see which way to go,
If you did not twinkle so.
When he stopped, it continued to echo in his mind.

Jason pulled one hand from his ear. The screaming and shouting eased. Voices and sounds of rushed movement echoed in the night air, but from which direction was hard to tell.

He sat up and leaned out from the fallen tree. He looked around, then stood.

Eyeing the darkness, Jason crept forward, one slow step after another. Near the grove's edge, he stopped and hid behind a wide trunk. Snow drifted straight down from the sky.

Pounding footsteps came from up the road. Jason crouched and held himself flat against the tree.

A man ran into view. His face was pale, eyes wide and panicked. He stopped across from Jason but looked back toward the river. He held out his hand and said a few quiet, urgent words. A woman hobbled up to the man and took his hand. Blonde, windblown hair hung in her face. She was crying. Mascara left dark tracks down her cheeks. The man rushed along again, dragging the woman behind him. She held her free hand against her thigh and struggled to keep up. Blood seeped between her fingers and down her leg. They moved out of sight, leaving the street empty, if only for a moment.

A man in a fitted suit walked through next. His dark hair was slicked back. His face lacked healthy color. A streak of something dark dripped down his chin and neck. Every few steps, he faltered, the slick soles of his dress shoes not offering much in the way of traction. He passed out of sight just as an old woman ambled into view. The hem of her fuzzy burgundy night coat flipped in the breeze. One of the rollers tucked in her graying hair hung loose. In matching tight jeans, tank tops, and cropped leather jackets, a pair of teenage girls dragged their feet through the snow behind her. Then came a man in greasy coveralls with bowed legs and another in a camo hunting jacket and matching hat. The crowd grew until it spanned the width of the street. That was when Jason noticed the air above them. Steam rose like smoke from an old train's stack, but it was more than their breath. He focused on their faces. Blood dripped from their ears and eyes. It dripped from their mouths, down their necks, and soaked into their clothes. The snow on the road beneath their feet became hard-packed and stained.

Jason stepped back from the tree and turned to run. His eye flinched up to a man towering over him. Like a policeman or soldier, the man wore a uniform, but it was not one Jason recognized. For a split second, he thought the uniformed man might be able to explain what was going on and get him to safety. That idea was quickly torn away when the man bared his blood-stained teeth and reached out with a mangled hand, missing the pinky and ring fingers. On his other hand, half the pointer finger was gone, and the middle limp at the point where it had broken.

Jason ducked and spun to evade, but the man caught the hood of his jacket and pulled him close. The uniformed man wrapped his hands around Jason's neck and forced him to the ground. He fought and scratched while Jason gasped for air. Tucking both legs to his chest, Jason kicked hard into the man's groin. The man recoiled, and his grip faltered. He tried to regain his grasp, but his hands were slick with blood, and Jason wriggled free.

Jason scrambled to his feet and ran. He weaved through the trees, working his way back to his hiding spot. Shadows moved along the edge of the grove, so he kept as low to the ground as possible. Breathing hard, Jason rounded a clutch of smaller growth and spotted the fallen tree. He stumbled and dove underneath, then pulled the leaf-covered blanket over his legs and backed in as far as he could.

Seconds later, he spotted movement between the branches. The man in the uniform lumbered through the trees, passing in and out of view. Jason held the edge of the blanket over his mouth to quiet the sound and visual signs of his breathing. The man stopped in front of the fallen tree. Jason could have reached out to touch him.

A gunshot shattered the silence, echoing from the west.

Another came from the north. The man turned in the direction of each. After a short pause, he stepped toward the street. His pace quickened, and soon, the man in the uniform was out of sight.

———

Della stared at the ceiling and held Waddles tight against her cheek. Wisps of her breath rose and faded above her. She would sometimes leave her mouth wide and hiss out columns of warm air, pretending she was breathing fire. Other times, she would pucker her lips and blow hard like she was shooting spitballs.

The flick of shuffling cards came from the kitchen. Della's mother and father had been playing games and at times, talking, for hours.

Della heard a clap come from outside her window, then another. She imagined someone popping balloons out in the middle of the night because there was nothing better to do. When she heard shouting, she sat up in bed. In the kitchen, the feet of a chair screeched back across the linoleum. Her father groaned as he stood.

Della came out of her room and stood at the entrance of the kitchen. On the table, two candles had burned down near the stubs. Stacks of cards were laid out in readiness for a new game. Empty beer cans and liquor bottles were piled up on the unoccupied side. Della's mother sat at the table but faced out. "What do you think it is?"

Everett leaned forward with his face close to the kitchen window. "Not sure." He stepped away and slicked back his unkempt hair. "Someone's wandering around out there. Think I'll go check it out."

"Are you sure?" Lori set her cards on the table and stood. "I'm sure it's just kids messing around."

"Maybe." Everett zipped his jacket and walked out the front door.

"Mommy?"

Lori spun with one hand flat against her chest. "Jesus." She closed her eyes and let out a sigh. "You scared me half to death, Della."

"Sorry." Della tightened her grip on Waddles.

Lori knelt down and put her hands on Della's shoulders. "What are you doing up?"

"Couldn't sleep. I heard noises."

"I know, baby. I'm sure it's nothing, but Daddy's gone out to see what's going on."

Della nodded and looked to the front door.

"Would you like a drink or anything?"

"Do we have any juice?"

"No, we're out. Sorry."

Della sniffed. "I'm okay then."

Lori frowned. She nodded, stood, and faced the front door with her arms crossed.

The noises they heard were muffled and indistinct. It could have been voices, or it could have been the wind. Della looked up to her mother. Lori held one hand to her mouth and chewed on the nail of her middle finger.

The stomping of heavy boots echoed on the front steps before the door flew open. Everett stumbled into the house. He slammed the door behind him and set the locks. His face was red, and his brow beaded with sweat. He unzipped his jacket and tracked snow through the kitchen as he made his way to the bathroom. "Make sure the back door is locked. Snuff those fuckin' candles too."

FIVE

Jason opened his eyes. The surrounding darkness was dense, like the ocean. He kept still, his breathing slow and measured. He laid on his side, facing out from the cover of the fallen tree. Only one eye saw past the blanket. A stray snowflake drifted to the ground. When he focused on its trajectory, he spotted something moving in the distance.

The cat held its head low, each step carefully placed. Its ears twitched to suss out every sound, and its eyes were full and wide. Jason could not tell if it was gray, brown, or perhaps a mixture of the two, but its coat was short and glossy. He could see dark stripes running from its back to the lighter fur on its belly. It brought to mind shows he had watched about tigers in the wild. Huge, powerful beasts. The kings of their own domain. Jason tried to draw a line between a tiger and a house cat in his mind. He wondered how much they really had in common.

Jason could not see what it was stalking or what it might be looking to avoid. He almost called out to it, but he found his throat too dry to speak. The cat walked on past the boy and wandered out of sight. Jason let his eyes rest straight ahead. He waited for any more stray house pets, but none came.

In the grove, it was dark and calm. Outside of the grove came sounds of conflict and struggle. Jason had lost count of the gunshots, but he heard at least two explosions while he was awake. One came from across the river, and one from near the south end of town.

Jason drew in a deep breath through his nose, then pushed it out. He licked at his teeth and swallowed, coaxing moisture across his tongue. One hand came out of the blanket and rubbed at the raised and broken skin on his neck, his thin fingernails breaking the fresh scabs enough for blood to seep through, then he closed his eyes and drifted off to sleep.

———

Lori stopped in the middle of the kitchen. Her shoulders stayed high, and her eyebrows drew together. She crossed her arms as she looked to the front door. "What are you doing up so early?"

Everett sat at the kitchen table. He leaned forward with his head in his hands. His right middle and pointer finger had the remnant of a lit cigarette caught between them. "Couldn't sleep."

"Any other problems out there?"

"Calmed down around sunrise."

"Do you want breakfast?"

"Did already. Not sittin' well."

"Oh." Lori raised an eyebrow. "Are those my smokes?"

Everett held out his hand and looked at the smoldering end. "Yeah."

Lori moved to stand beside Everett. "Are you out?"

"Think I have more in the van. I'll head out in a bit."

Lori bent down, looked in Everett's eyes, and held the back of her hand against his forehead. "You feeling okay?"

Everett shoved her hand away. "No, I'm not feelin' okay. Enough with all the questions already."

Lori wiped her hands against her pants and re-crossed her arms. Everett pushed back from the table and stood. He took an open bottle of ibuprofen from the table and shook out two pills into his hand. After tossing the pills in his mouth, he picked up an almost empty glass of water to drain it. Everett swallowed, then exhaled hard. He ran a hand through his hair as he turned away from the table. "I'm going to lie down for a bit. Don't bother me."

Everett zigzagged down the hall and disappeared through the bedroom door.

"Mommy?"

Lori flinched, and her arms tightened across her body. Turning toward the living room, she saw Della leaning around the partition. "You really need to stop doing that." She released a sharp breath. "What the hell are you doing in there anyway?"

"Waiting for Daddy to go. He's not in a good mood."

Lori looked toward the hall. "Yeah." She turned back to Della. "Have you had breakfast?"

"No. We don't have anything."

Lori frowned. "Course we do. There's cereal and—"

"But we have no milk."

"You can get by without milk for one more day."

"Does that mean the lights are coming back?"

Lori shrugged. "Sure. Can't last forever, right?"

Della smiled.

Images of the man in the uniform flashed across Jason's mind, vast and distorted like reflections in a funhouse mirror. His mouth filled with teeth like the tips of razor blades. Dark, empty sockets, like bottomless pits, occupied the space where his eyes should have been.

Jason cracked one eyelid open. The vision of the uniformed man flooded with burning light until it disappeared. Jason opened his other eye, but only enough to see. The world around him was gray and depressing, but still, he had trouble adjusting to the glare.

He sat up, pushed the blanket back, then stretched his arms out and looked around. Seeing no signs of movement, he crawled out from under the tree and brushed at his pants as he stood. Unzipping his jacket, Jason coughed into the open air.

The grove of trees was still. Nothing could be heard other than the breeze pushing through the higher branches and sparrows making small noises as they hopped from tree to tree. Paths had been worn in the snow toward the street. Otherwise, it looked much the same as when he arrived the day before.

Jason kicked a leaf half covered in snow, then licked at the taught and cracked skin on his lips. What little saliva he mustered stung as his tongue drew across. He turned to the road and watched the ground as he walked.

At the edge of the trees, Jason stopped. He looked back and forth, then sat. The street had been worn smooth but was uneven. Trails of blood left pink halos in the snow. A body laid face down in the middle.

The woman's skin looked as dull as the sky. Her arms were straight by her side as if she froze mid-stride and fell like a stick into the snow. Mud, or possibly blood, soaked the hem of her long, gray coat. Her stockings were torn, and one of her shoes was missing. Her hair reminded Jason of his mother's. He watched her for a moment longer, then focused on another body further along. It was twisted and might have been missing part of an arm. It was hard to tell through the torn clothing and remaining ragged flesh.

Jason leaned forward and adjusted to sit on his boots. He crossed his arms and leaned into the trunk of a small tree. Looking down to a patch of snow beside him, he licked at his dry lips again. Focused on the fresh snow, Jason pulled the glove from his right hand and dug in to take a handful. He packed it into a loose ball about the size of an apple and took a bite. The cold shock was less than expected. In fact, it felt amazing. Jason spread his tongue over his lips, letting the excess moisture dribble down his chin. He took another bite and settled forward to watch the road.

With the portion nearly gone, Jason scooped more fresh snow and built the ball back up. He packed it down, then pulled out a stray blade of grass, stood, and walked back into the grove.

Everett sat in the living room, staring at the blank TV screen. His fingernails dug into the arms of the chair, and one knee bounced like a seismograph recording the end of the world.

Lori leaned against the wall by the kitchen with her arms folded across her chest. "What can I do?"

Everett kept his eyes fixed on the TV. "Ain't nothin' to do."

Lori lowered her head and bit at her lip. "You want a beer or somethin'? A smoke?"

"Ain't no smokes left and no fuckin' beer either."

"We could go ask the Duffy's if they have any to spare?"

"I ain't askin' that holier-than-thou piece of shit for nothin'."

"What about the neighbors on the other side?"

"They ain't much better."

"Should we maybe go to your sister's? They have a camper and everything. Must be better setup than we are."

"That's all the way across town. How the hell you think we're gonna get there?"

Lori shrugged her shoulders and looked up through her bangs. "You wanna, you know…"

Everett's leg stopped jumping. He turned his head to Lori and scowled. "What the fuck is wrong with you? You think I've got a hit for you or somethin'? That what you think?"

"No, I—"

"Get outta here."

"Come on, Ev."

Everett pushed forward in his chair and bared his teeth. "Get. The fuck. Out of here. *Now*."

Lori dropped her hands to her side and turned to go. At the transition between the kitchen and the living room, Della stood with a blanket over her back and her eyes wide. Lori reached out and put a hand on her shoulder to move her away. Della made a soft noise as she shuffled aside.

Everett's face twitched. He tilted his head and glared at the girl. "The fuck did you just say to me?"

Della looked to her mother, then to Everett. She slowly shook her head.

Everett raised up in his chair. "No, you said somethin'. Tell me what you said."

Lori stepped in front of Della. "Ev, she didn't say anything."

"The fuck she didn't." Everett stood on shaky legs. "Come here and say it to my face, you little bitch."

Della clutched the blanket and pushed against her mother's leg. Her lower lip trembled, and tears welled in her eyes.

Lori held a hand toward Everett and inched Della out of the room. "Everett, she didn't say anything. Not a word. Just sit on down. I'll—I'll find something to make it better. I promise."

Everett stood with his fists clenched and one eye twitching. A tiny bit of saliva dripped from the corner of his mouth. He watched Lori and Della back out of the room with his breath sharp and his teeth grinding together. When they were out of sight, Everett flopped back in his chair. He grabbed at his hair, bending forward with his legs wide and screamed at the floor.

———

Jason rolled onto his back and blinked. He fanned the collar of his jacket to push cold air against his skin and damp shirt. He rolled out from under the fallen tree and stood. As he straightened his back, he winced. His muscles screamed at him to be still.

The sky to the east faded from stone gray to charcoal. Snow began to fall again. Jason held the palm of his hand against his temple to calm the pounding in his brain as he looked up. He dropped his head and held himself tight. His stomach grumbled, but he didn't feel hungry. Everything felt wrong.

The lullaby played through his mind again, this time unprompted. Jason looked under the fallen tree toward his backpack. He wiped a tear from his cheek. His breath caught, and his body shook as he tried to hold back the emotion fighting to be released.

———

"What was that?"

Everett turned in his chair. "It's starting again. Put the candles out."

Lori licked her fingers and pinched the wicks of the candles on the coffee table. Sitting back on the couch, she pulled her legs up beside her. "What do we do?"

Everett rubbed at his forehead. He mumbled his response. "I don't know."

They sat without speaking, listening to the wind blow and the snow click against the windows.

Della ran into the living room and jumped up on the couch beside Lori. She wrapped her arms around her mother and buried her face in her neck.

"What's wrong, baby?"

"Someone's in the backyard."

"What are you talking about?"

"I heard something. I think it was the back gate."

Everett pursed his lips, and his face lost what little color it had. He rose to his feet and walked to the window. With one hand cupped against the glass, he stared into the darkness. Everett turned and zipped up his jacket, then walked through the kitchen and out the back door. Lori looked to Della, pushed herself up off the couch, and followed after Everett.

Lori stepped onto the back porch. Della followed close behind, wrapping her arms around Lori's waist. Lori set a hand on Della's shoulder but kept her eyes focused on Everett.

Everett stopped at the depression in the middle of the yard. He turned all ways, scanning for signs of movement. The back gate had been forced open. One of the boards, broken clean off, stuck out of the snow nearby. Trails in the snow led around to the corner of the yard.

Everett called out. "Where you at, you piece of shit. You want trouble? You're in the right place." Everett lifted the hem of his jacket and took a folded knife from the sheath on his belt. He flipped the blade open and held it out. "Come on and get it."

For a moment, the falling snow was the only thing that changed. Raising her head, Della pointed into the shadows. "Mom, look."

The blanket on the fort pulled to one side, and a figure emerged. The figure stood to face Everett. The stream of heat from their breath wafted up and drifted away.

Lori tightened her grip on Della's shoulder and held the other hand over her mouth. "Oh my God. Jason?"

Everett looked back at Lori, then to the shadow standing across the yard. "You little son of a bitch." He adjusted the grip on his knife. "Get your ass over here."

Lori pushed away and started down the front steps. Della reached out and grabbed at the sleeve of her coat. "No. Wait."

Jason was still at first. He turned his head to check behind him, then faced forward and walked out of the shadows. Only a t-shirt and jeans protected him from the cold and snow. Faint haze drifted from his exposed skin. Dark stains ran down from his mouth to his shirt and over his narrow chest, and blood left tracks from the corners of his eyes. Jason stopped shy of Everett by three or four paces. His arms were limp at his sides, his head low and cocked at an angle.

"I knew you'd be back." Everett turned his head to spit but kept his eyes locked on the boy. "Think you're a big man settin' out on your own? Guess we all know exactly what you are now, don't we?"

Jason raised his head and focused his bloodshot eyes on Everett.

Everett swallowed as he took a half step back.

Jason bared his teeth. He planted one foot and launched forward. A fine mist of blood sprayed as he screamed and flew into Everett's chest. Jason straddled his father as they toppled into the snow. He punched and scratched at Everett's face.

With the knife still in his hand, Everett hooked his arm to wrap over Jason's neck. Immediately, the boy turned and bit down on Everett's hand. Everett shouted and dropped the knife onto his own chest.

Time stopped as they focused on the glistening blade. Jason reached out first. Taking the wood handle in his small hand, he raised the knife over his head. Jason screeched like a rabid dog straining at its lead and brought the knife down with every bit of force he could manage.

Everett flipped his head to one side. The blade grazed his cheek and split the lobe of his ear. The second missed. The third caught him on the neck. Everett grabbed at the back of Jason's shirt and strained to pull him away.

Jason lifted the knife again and plunged it into Everett's shoulder, just below the collarbone. Everett folded in on himself and cried out. Wrapping both hands around the blade's handle, Jason let a primal scream loose, inches from Everett's face, then put all his weight down on it.

With the hilt buried, Jason sat back. His chest heaved, arms limp at his sides. Everett moaned and brought a hand up to where the knife stuck out of his body. His eyes fluttered, and he bucked to roll away from the boy. Jason stood and stepped to one side. He did not look down at Everett, sunk into the snow and surrounded by the spray of blood. Instead, he lifted his head and focused on his mother and sister.

Lori held Della close with one arm and wrapped the other over the girl's face. Della shook and cried. Lori's chin quivered, and her eyes filled with moisture as she watched Jason.

The boy held his mother's gaze. He watched tears track down her gaunt face. Jason let out a deep breath and broke away. Keeping his head down, he pushed through the snow toward the front gate.

Lori released Della and hopped down the steps into the yard. When she came around the end of the house, Jason leaned against the front gate. He forced it open enough to get through, then walked between the vehicles and down the driveway. Without looking back, he turned along the street and disappeared into the storm.

———

Everett opened his right eye. The left remained shut, bloodied and swollen. Blurry flakes drifted across a background of deep gray. They landed on his face and melted, but he paid them no mind. He winced as he reached up to his shoulder, then coughed open mouthed.

The knife handle occupied the far corner of his vision.

Everett looked down and rested his fingers around it. After drawing in a deep breath, he tightened his grip and pulled. The sensation was immediate. Cold and biting. He rolled on his side and fought to quiet the scream rising in his throat. Everett pushed the hand holding the knife handle into the snow while keeping the opposite arm tight to his body. On the third attempt, he righted himself to sit. He tossed the knife to one side and rose on his knees.

Snow swirled around him. It softened the worn paths across the yard. The screen door of the house swung about in the breeze. He reached out for a handful of snow, squeezed it flat, and held it to his swollen eye.

Sounds of violence came from all around. Raised voices and crying out. A rifle shot echoed somewhere in the distance. A brief moment of calm settled before an explosion two blocks over ripped it away.

Everett looked up to the ominous glow in the sky. As it faded, he removed the packed snow from his eye. It was translucent and stained red. Everett tossed it to one side, inhaled deeply, coughed again, then pushed himself to stand.

He hunched forward and moved through the snow to the back door. Everett pulled himself up the stairs with his good arm. He stepped inside, hooked his foot on the bottom of the door, and flicked it closed.

"Lori, get your ass in here."

At the kitchen counter, Everett spun the roll of paper towel on its wooden spindle and ripped off a handful of sheets. He bunched them up, lifted his jacket to place them over the wound in his shoulder, then turned to the room.

A cluster of candles occupied the middle of the kitchen table. The sinks were level with dirty dishes, but the counter on either side was clear. The cupboard door under the sink had been propped open.

"Lori?"

He waited but received no response. Down the hall, he leaned through the bedroom doorway but found it empty. He came down the hallway and into the living room. It was empty as well. Stopping, Everett looked toward the half-melted snow that had been tracked to the front door.

"Goddamn it."

Everett stepped to the entryway and opened the door. With one foot on the porch, he traced two sets of tracks winding down the steps and out to the street. Everett stepped back into the house and slammed the door. He clenched his teeth and kicked at it with the flat of his boot.

"Stupid bitch."

He stumbled back and raised his hand to his shoulder. His jaw trembled, and his voice came soft. "Fuck you, then."

Everett wiped at his eyes, and his hand came away tinted red. Rubbing his hand on his pant leg, he turned toward the kitchen.

On his way to the sink, he stepped in a bit of slush, and his legs splayed out. Through gritted teeth, Everett swore under his breath and steadied his footing. Breathing in and out through his nose, he paused before continuing. At the sink, he reached for the lever on the faucet. A thin stream of water trickled out before it ran dry. Everett pushed the tap's lever down and up again. No water came. He wrenched it until it spun from his hand. A growl rose in his throat. *"Fuck."*

Everett slammed his closed fist on the counter and kicked the cupboard door shut. He ripped a few more sheets from the paper towel roll and laid them flat on the counter. He took a glass from the sink that was a third full of water, upended it on the paper towel, and dropped the glass back in the sink. He squeezed the wet paper towel to distribute the moisture to all corners, then took it flat in his hand and wiped his face.

Everett drew in a sharp breath as he wiped down his neck and the side of his head. He winced when he grazed the cut on his ear. After the pain had dulled, he dabbed at it. The towel came away fresh with blood. Everett balled up the wet paper towel and threw it at the backsplash. Tearing off a new sheet, he held it against his ear as he walked toward the bathroom.

SIX

Everett opened his eyes to the sound of a windowpane shaking in the wind. He held his hand along his brow and squinted into the dim light. The window framed falling snow backed by a never-ending dull gray sky. It was a new day, and for the time being, the outside world remained quiet.

Everett pushed the blankets down to his waist, closed his eyes, and rolled to his opposite side. The pillow had a dark ring of blood and was damp with sweat. He swallowed, and his tongue stuck to the roof of his mouth. When he cleared his throat, it sent him into a fit of coughing.

Everett sat up and wiped his mouth. He leaned forward on his elbows while he worked to calm his breathing. With one final exhale, he raised his head, then swung his legs out of bed to stand. He scratched at his scalp as he lurched out of the room.

In the bathroom, Everett stood in front of the toilet and unzipped his pants. He closed his eyes and let out a slow breath as his bladder drained. When the flow stopped, he shook and did up his pants. Leaning in close to the mirror,

Everett pulled down on his bruised eyelid. It was crusted with blood in the creases, but the swelling had subsided some. He could at least open it enough to see again.

Everett turned right out of the bathroom and continued down the hall to the kitchen. At the sink, he pulled a glass close to him. Two ceramic bowls with worn floral patterns under the rim sat to the left of the sink, each half filled with slushy water. He took one bowl in both hands and lifted it over the glass. His hands shook as it neared empty, spilling water onto the counter that ran down the cupboards to the floor. With the last drop consumed, he set the bowl down and pushed it to one side.

Everett licked at his dry lips and reached for an open bottle of ibuprofen on the other side of the sink. He shook out three pills, popped them into his mouth, then lifted the glass of water and gulped it down. His hand with the glass crashed down on the countertop. He bit down and twisted his head away. When the pain from the cold subsided, he repeated the process with the second bowl.

Everett picked up both bowls and moved to the back door. He craned his neck to look through the small square window. Satisfied the backyard was unoccupied, he tucked the bowls in the crook of his good arm, drew back the deadbolt, and opened the door. In only his socks, Everett walked down the porch steps and into the yard. He watched the fence line as he scooped snow into the bowls and packed it flat. With the bowls stacked, one on top of the other, he shuffled back inside.

Everett set the bowls on the kitchen counter. He locked the back door, leaving a faint trail of snow as he continued to the bedroom.

SEVEN

Everett woke with a start. The sheets and pillows had been pushed off onto the floor. His limbs were at odd angles. One corner of the fitted sheet had pulled off. It was bunched up and soaked with sweat. The curtain at the window billowed out as cold air pushed into the room, showing a darkened sky beyond.

Everett groaned as he sat up and leaned back on his hands. His breathing was shallow and ragged. He ran his tongue over his cracked lips, then rolled to the edge of the bed to get up.

He walked down the hall to the bathroom, holding his pants up by his belt. At the toilet, he unzipped and waited. Little more than a trickle fell to the edge of the bowl. Everett's breath rattled. He coughed as he did up his pants. He cinched his belt to a new notch and moved out into the hall.

When he entered the kitchen, Everett pulled the damp shirt away from his chest. His bare feet stuck to the linoleum as he walked to the sink. He stared at the bowls. The vapor from his breath pushed out in front of him in short puffs. Lifting one of the bowls to his lips, he slurped and gulped until it was empty. He ran his hand down his mouth, then lifted the second. Halfway through, he bucked forward. Everett choked and spit water as he fumbled the bowl to the counter. With one hand on his stomach, he screamed out and bent in half.

He breathed through the pain enough to right himself. Growling through bared teeth, he lifted the bowl by the rim and threw it across the room. It hit the bottom of the opposite wall and shattered. Pieces fanned out in all directions from the dent in the paneling. Everett clenched his fists and shouted. *"Goddamn it."*

He took the glass from the counter and pitched it in the same direction. Grabbing the second bowl with both hands, he smashed it straight down.

Everett stormed through the kitchen, paying no attention to the shards of porcelain and glass as he tracked through it. In the middle of the living room, his knees buckled and his footing faltered. He grabbed at his stomach as he folded over.

"What the fuck—"

Holding himself with one arm and crawled to the couch. Everett rested his arm on the edge of the seat and set his forehead on top. Saliva dripped from his lips, and his chest heaved with deep and uneven breaths. Stifling a scream, he clutched at his shirt and pulled it away from his body. He lifted his head, and his throat caught. Everett's bloodshot eyes spread wide, and his jaw fell slack. Slamming his forehead onto his arm, his torso curled in. He gagged and spit out a stream of dark mess, thick like cold motor oil. His body seized again as the sickness continued to flow.

When it eased, Everett pinched his lips and spit. He watched as the mess pooled and soaked into the carpet.

Irritation in his eyes made him blink. He released his shirt and wiped one eye. His fingers came away stained glossy crimson.

Shaking and unsteady, Everett raised his head to look out the living room window. The falling snow glowed like static as it fell from the sky. He could hear it click against the glass and siding and put pressure on the joists as it built up on the roof. The front door vibrated and shook with the burden of the wind. Everett could not take his eyes from it. All of his senses spiked to heights he had never known before.

He spit again, pushed himself to stand, and staggered to the door. He reached out for the handle but froze. Every line and detail in his hand stood out. He cocked his head and twisted his lips. Focusing on the door, Everett turned the handle and pushed it open. He raised his face into the chilled air as he walked onto the porch.

He stopped at the end of the driveway and looked along the street. A man in an open bathrobe and panda slippers shuffled along a path that had been worn down the middle. The open wound on his forehead dripped down his face, mixing with the dark, crusted blood from his eyes before trailing down his face and neck.

The man stopped and turned to Everett. They watched each other. The man clenched and loosened his jaw. Everett scanned the man's face and the vapor rising from his skin. The wind shifted, wafting a hint of copper and rank death. Finally breaking his gaze, the man turned back to the path and continued up the road. Everett relaxed his shoulders and followed.

As they walked, Everett lifted his eyes toward the falling snow. Tree branches bent and creaked in the incessant wind. Delicate ice crystals flared bright and crackled as they bobbed and drifted. Everett's upper lip curled, and he lowered his gaze.

The man in the bathrobe came to the end of the street, then diverted north onto a two-lane road. A loose group of five people moved ahead of them as Everett followed. All carried the same slow gait. Each had varying degrees of damage to their person, but Everett had no issue picking out the details even from a block away and in the dark. Mangled hands missing fingers. Shredded clothes exposing torn skin. Twisted legs and the slight shift with each step, giving a glimpse of broken bones underneath.

He looked past the group. The sense of something deep in the distance lulled him. It focused him and urged him on. Keeping a steady but careful pace with his bare feet on the packed snow, Everett walked on.

As he neared the end of the block, a scream rang out. Everett held a hand against his ear and scowled as the sharp tone pierced his skull.

A woman in a puffy blue jacket and a thick knit cap ran out into the road. Pale and frantic, she wielded a small axe at her side. Three people followed the woman out from the side street, fixated on her like predators tracking prey.

The woman froze when she saw Everett and the others moving toward her. The first of the group of five, a young man in a baggy t-shirt and jeans, launched forward. The woman's face twisted, and she swung straight out with the axe. It caught the man in the neck, tearing a deep gash through his Adam's apple. He slowed and grabbed at his neck with one hand. He reached for the woman with the other, but his legs lost their strength, and he fell short.

Turning as the group of three neared, the woman raised the axe and brought it down into the clavicle of the man in the lead. He staggered but remained upright. The woman pulled on the axe, but it stuck deep. She looked back just as she was overrun and pushed to the ground by the group on the main road.

The woman's screams shook Everett's temples as he sprinted ahead. He pushed past the man in the panda slippers and forced himself into the melee. The commotion eased as he clawed through the mass of bodies on the ground. When the group dispersed, the woman laid still. Bright, wide eyes contrasted the dark gore streaking her face. Everett sensed her heartbeat, faint as it was. The others fell into a steady gait and continued along the street. Everett paused to look up to the horizon, then followed.

The group moved north along the river. Everett stayed at the back, with only the man in the robe behind him. Soon, they moved out of the denser parts of Fort Erie and into more open spaces. The well-worn paths narrowed and, at times, disappeared as people drifted and found their own way.

The abrasive noises and chaos in town faded. Even though it could not be seen, the sensation pulling at Everett felt stronger and the direction clear as the group diverted west. He kept enough distance to see the person in front of him through the fireworks of falling snow, but no closer.

They walked on without interaction until the wind and the snow calmed. It was then that a shimmering light caught Everett's attention. It stood out like a candle in a dark room, even though it had to be almost a kilometer away. The light scratched at his eyes. Balling his hands into fists, he looked back and forth along the path. The others had noticed as well.

Everett flinched at the sound of a gunshot. With the second, the woman ahead of him with dark, stringy hair and a patchy complexion pressed her hands against her head and exhaled hard. She left the path, pushing straight through the snowdrifts toward the light. Everett squinted at the man in the robe. He stomped off behind the woman, losing his slippers within the first few steps.

Everett grabbed at the hair on his head. His teeth ground together, and he spit blood as he growled. Lifting his feet high, he hopped through the deep snow to catch up with the others.

The trio eventually moved out from the drifts into gaping tire ruts carved in a narrow road. The light grew brighter, and the noises sharper. More shots rang out. The group quickened their pace.

A ring of houses with a fire burning at a clearing in the middle was situated just beyond a bend in the road. Two men stood on either side of the fire. One in a thick hunting jacket held a rifle with a wood grip and stock. He scowled beneath a mess of sandy hair and a bent, dirty cap. His eyes moved in all directions to scan the darkness. The other had red hair, unkempt from days without rest, and the beginning of a beard. A camouflage-painted shotgun rested against the shoulder of his unbuttoned jacket. His body pointed away from the road as if prepared to run, and his breath came in short bursts.

The tempo of their heartbeats and the number of days since they had last bathed became clear as Everett neared. The rage and the need to quiet the abuse on his senses rose in his body with each step.

He fell in behind the man in the robe. The woman advanced beside him in the opposite rut. When Everett raised one hand to shield his eyes from the blinding light of the fire, a shot rang out, and the man in the robe fell to one knee. Bits of meat and bone sprayed into Everett's face, and his hearing reduced to a constricted whine. He looked to see one of the man's shoulders reduced to something resembling hamburger and the arm hanging limp.

Everett felt the concussion of the second shot. The woman's head jerked back before she toppled to the ground.

As the man raised his head and struggled to stand, he took a round to the face, then slumped forward and finally laid still.

Everett clawed at the air and screamed, but it was little more than a dull roar in his head. The man with the shotgun shifted to reload. Everett focused on him and vaulted over the broken body of the man in the bathrobe. As he reached the clearing, he felt the action of a rifle from his right.

Time slowed. A shockwave washed over Everett's body. Next came a pinch at his jaw. Flesh tore. Bones and teeth shattered. Finally, the hot slug of metal touched his spinal cord. Before shock could register in his nervous system, the bullet passed through, and all sensation went with it.

Thank you for reading!

Reviews are extremely important to indie authors. They help us hone our craft and find new readers. If you enjoyed this book, please consider sharing your thoughts on Amazon, Goodreads, or BookBub.

———

———

Also by Shane Kroetsch

This and That but Mostly the Other
Surviving the Storm (The Storm Series Book 2)
Chasing the Storm (The Storm Series Book 3)

ACKNOWLEDGMENTS

With my last project, I had a lot of people to acknowledge, because I had a lot of help. It was an amazing experience. One, in fact, I wouldn't change for anything. This time around, things are different. I've been striving for fewer moving parts in my life, and maybe that's effecting the business of writing as well. I'm very proud of this effort, and I hope it finds at least some small amount of acceptance. Anyway, here we go.

To my constant and irrational fear of zombies, thank you. I could not have done this without you.

To the world at large, full of terrible things and shitty people, thank you for helping make my fiction scarier because it's not so fictional.

To my constant need to be better, for Christ's sake, calm down a little. Just a little though.

To Kaleigh, Wonder Twin powers, activate!

To me, good job little buddy.

To you, dear reader, thank you. While I like to think I'm doing this for myself, it helps the plans for world domination if there are people who enjoy it and want to pay for it.

ABOUT THE AUTHOR

To date, Shane has released a collection of short fiction, a zombie outbreak trilogy, and been featured in a growing number of anthologies. In his spare time, he builds projects out of old junk, paints watercolor blanket ghosts, and shakes his butt while the vinyl spins.

The best way to keep up to date with his writing shenanigans, including his current work in progress, and access exclusive short stories is to subscribe at www.ShaneKroetsch.com.